MORNING STAR

"Time for bed!"
Moon called to her stars,
as Sun began to rise.

Little Star pretended
that he couldn't hear her.

Moon called again.
"Come on,
or you'll be too tired
to shine again
tomorrow night."

Little Star sighed.
He *did* want to see Sun
shining on the world
beneath him.

Sun was yawning
and peeping up
over the horizon.

"It never looks so pretty
at night,"
thought Little Star.

"Little Star!" called Moon,
and Little Star knew
he had to follow her.

"I have to find a way
of hiding in the sky,"
he said to himself.
"Then Moon won't miss me."

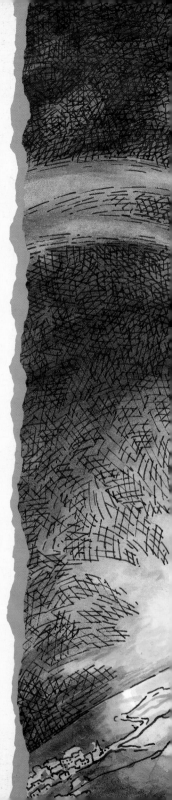

Next evening,
when Moon called the stars out,
Little Star hid
in a dark part
of the sky.

There, he twinkled
all on his own
for a long time.

At last,
he saw Sun peering sleepily
over the rim
of the world.

Moon and all the stars
slowly disappeared.

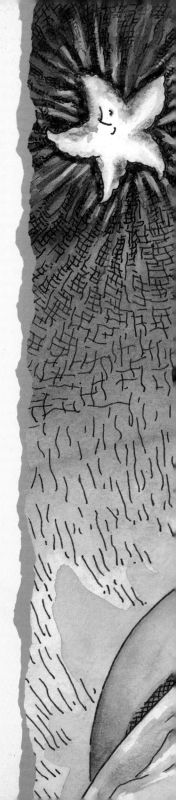

"Heigh ho!" called Sun,
when he saw Little Star.
"What have we here?
A little lost star?"

Little Star was frightened.
"No," he said,
in a small voice,
"I just wanted
to see the world
when you shine
your brightest."

"And so you shall,"
said Sun.
"You can keep me company
today."

Sun and Little Star
talked and roamed
across the blue sky all day.

In the evening,
when Moon and all the stars
ran into the sky,
Little Star hurried
to join them.

"Where have you been?"
asked Moon, anxiously.

But before Little Star
could answer,
Sun called to Moon.

"Moon! Let him stay later
than the rest,"
he said,
"long enough for me
to chat with him."
And with that,
Sun slipped down
behind the edge of the world,
and the sky grew dark.

From then on,
Little Star stayed in the sky
to talk to Sun.

And if you get up early
one morning,
look up into the sky.
You might see Little Star there.

He'll be twinkling
as brightly as a diamond,
while he waits for Sun.

But he isn't called Little Star now.
Sun and Moon gave him a new name.

They called him
MORNING STAR.